DESERT KINGS

A Christmas Wedding

By Jennifer Lewis

This is a work of fiction. Names, characters, places, and
incidents either are the product of the author's imagination
or are used fictitiously. Any resemblance to actual persons,
living or dead, events, or locales is entirely coincidental

1

A Christmas celebration in the desert had seemed like such a good idea at the time. "Sweetheart, don't touch that!" Samantha swooped forward to grab a big hand-blown glass ornament from her niece's tiny hands. "It's very fragile. Not safe."

Little Parsia's lip quivered.

"I'm sorry, honey. It's not for playing with. It's just supposed to look pretty." What was she thinking? In New York she'd just bought a tiny tree for her apartment and cut out some paper snowflakes to hang on it. For her first Christmas here in the palace she'd gone a bit nuts. "Check this out. It's called tinsel." She pressed a glittery snake into the confused girl's arms.

Parsia looked doubtful. "It's prickly."

Sam placed the glass globe, hanging from a menacingly sharp hook, high out of the child's reach on a branch of decorative holly.

"I don't remember Christmas being this dangerous when I was a kid," she said to her sister-in-law Aliyah, whose two sweet daughters were at least half the reason she'd gone so over the top with decorations and festivities. "Next year will be smoother, I promise."

"It's all very…exciting." Aliyah smiled sweetly. She was so shy it was hard to have a conversation with her. Sam's halting grasp of the local language didn't help. "I think it's a lovely holiday."

"A lot of countries celebrate Christmas these days." Was Sam trying to reassure Aliyah or herself? "You see decorations even in places like Tokyo and Dubai."

When she'd realized they didn't celebrate Christmas here in Ubar, she'd decided to go large. Osman had liked the idea of combining their wedding with the seasonal celebration. She'd convinced herself that ordering decorations from all over the world would be fun and festive and make all their guests feel at home.

Right now it was the day before their Christmas Eve wedding, people were arriving from the airport and everything seemed on the brink of imploding. The mistletoe she'd ordered from Austria was invading all the trees in the garden, unexpected butterflies were everywhere— fluttering through the hallways of the palace, in people's hair and on their plates.

Tinsel and ribbon were a fire hazard with all the open torches that lit the palace at night, and now the blown-glass ornaments she'd ordered from Italy were threatening the safety of Aliyah's children.

"We really shouldn't leave eggnog out on the table in the dining room. It'll spoil in the heat," she called to one of the waiters. The staff meant well but they had no idea how Christmas worked and hung all the stars upside down. Sam felt like the Grinch going around fixing everything.

"Don't worry, sweetheart." Osman materialized

behind her like a genie, his deep voice a balm to her nerves.

"It's hard not to! We have three hundred guests arriving and the place is in chaos."

"They're here to celebrate our wedding, and Zadir and Veronica's. They probably won't even notice the decorations."

"You say that because you're from Ubar, where Christmas doesn't exist. Where the closest thing to Santa is a djinn who leaves figs in peoples shoes."

"Figs are a delicious treat." He pulled her into his big, strong arms.

"Not if you're used to candy canes." She felt her stress levels dropping as he pulled her close. "But you're right. It's about friends and family, not getting the decorations perfect. I don't know what's come over me. I don't usually turn into Martha Stewart at Christmastime. When I was a kid, my family brought out the same garish fake tree and decorations year after year and it was just fine."

"I know what you need." Osman's low voice challenged her as he bumped his chest against hers and shot her a sultry glance.

Desire crept through her and she tried to stop a smile spreading across her face. "Tempting, but we'll have to save it for later. We have guests to greet."

"They can wait." He pressed his lips to hers and heat flashed through her.

She pulled herself back with difficulty, and sighed. "Now you're just tormenting me. You know we can't just disappear off to our bedroom."

"Says who? I'm the king around here." His green eyes sparkled with mischief.

"You do have a point."

"Sam!!" A shriek made her jump and spin around.

"Mom!" She detached herself from Osman and hurried across the stone floor before her mom could skid on it in her high heels. "I'm so glad you made it." She inhaled her mom's signature scent—expensive Dior perfume—and wrapped her arms around her for a hug. Which made her notice something very strange. "Mom…" She pulled back and looked down. "Are you...?"

"Pregnant. Yes, darling! Isn't it wild?"

Sam stared. She'd been trying to get pregnant for the last four months, and nothing. Now her mom was having a baby. "But you're fifty-two." This didn't compute.

"Shhh. Darling. That's nonsense. I'm forty-six, just like Halle Berry was when she had—"

"I'm your daughter. I know what year you were born." *Oh dear.* Already they were falling back into their familiar roles. Sam as the boringly organized and practical daughter and her mom the charismatic and kooky star of stage and screen. "But seriously, I'm thrilled for you. What a surprise." She searched for her father in the crowd. "What have you done with dad? It is his, I hope?"

Her mom's laugh boomed through the arches. "Darling, you're such a card. Get out of the way so I can hug that handsome husband of yours."

Osman gracefully accepted the perfumed embrace, while Sam's father ambled forward, still handsome and dashing in a cream summer suit, his thick hair kept brown by Hollywood's expert colorists. "Hiya sweetie. Quite a bash you have going on here."

She smiled as she kissed him on the cheek. "I'm so glad you could come, dad. I know it's hard for you guys to get away at this time of year." Her parents often appeared in Christmas Spectaculars. "It means a lot to me."

"I wouldn't miss my little girl's wedding for the world."

"She's already married, darling." Her mom scolded him. "We've missed it."

Osman shook her dad's hand warmly. "We're man and wife by Ubarite convention, because I claimed her during our annual marriage rites, but this is the first proper celebration we've had."

"And it looks like quite a shindig." Her mom swatted at a red and green butterfly that tried to land on the tip of her nose. "Who are all these people?"

"Osman and his brothers have friends from all over the world. You're having a baby. That's amazing."

"It was your mother's idea." Her dad grinned sheepishly. "She always said she still had the body of a twenty-five year old, and now she's proving it to the world."

You had to laugh. "You guys are awesome. And I really mean that. Come get some eggnog before it curdles."

"I don't think I've ever been so nervous in my life." Ronnie Baxter applied lip gloss with shaking hands in the bedroom she shared with her almost-husband Zadir.

"Why?" The look of concern on his handsome face made her laugh.

"Not because I'm getting cold feet about the wedding." She squeezed his hand. "But it would mean so much to me if my parents were here and yet I'm worried they're going to ruin everything."

"Why would they do that?"

Ronnie bit her lip. "You know I really want my dad to give me away, right?"

"Of course, that's tradition."

"And since I've been to four of his weddings, he pretty much had to agree." She tried to smile. "But I didn't tell my mom he was coming."

"What? Why not?" His surprise reminded her how little they knew about each other.

"Because she's not over him divorcing her twenty-some years ago. She's still in love with him."

"And he's arriving with his fourth wife."

"Fifth. And she's my age." She cringed a little every time she remembered that.

Zadir pretended to wince. "Ouch."

"I told you my family was screwed up."

"Mine too, remember? At least your dad didn't have your mom killed so he could remarry." He stroked her cheek, and the warmth of the gesture soothed her.

Ronnie exhaled. "True! Thank heaven for small mercies. Still, I'm worried she'll make a scene, or just turn around and leave. She's a bit of a diva. She was a professional singer, after all."

Zadir moved up behind her and laid a soft kiss on her cheek. "Everything will work out fine in the end."

She smiled for a second—his kisses usually had that effect on her—but her doubts lingered. "Will it? Everything seems so nuts lately. I'm happy that I've moved across the world to be with you, but the insurgents are still causing trouble, our house plans keep hitting snags and Sam's big fat crazy Christmas has turned the palace into a madhouse. Where have all these butterflies come from?"

A butterfly was perched right on the bedpost. And another two on the window shutters. "You can't even go to the bathroom lately without a butterfly watching."

Zadir laughed. "Butterflies flourish wherever there's a source of the food they live on. I think it's the mistletoe Sam ordered to make garlands. It seems to be so perfectly suited to the environment here that it's reproducing like a virus."

"I suppose there are worse things that butterflies in your hair. Or mistletoe in your date palms."

"Unquestionably." His soft blue gaze rested gently on her face, and the tension slipped from her body as he slid his arms around her waist. "Now that you're here with me I find I can't worry about anything very much."

His lips lowered over hers, sparking heat low in her belly. She sucked in a breath. "As long as we end up married, everything will be fine."

"Exactly. I can't wait to see you in your dress."

"I can't wait to see it myself."

"What do you mean?" His eyes widened.

"The seamstress took my measurements three weeks ago and that was the last I heard. Sam keeps insisting she's on top of everything and since her plate is so full lately I don't want to bug her about it."

Zadir lifted a brow. "What if she's forgotten?"

"Then I guess I'll just have to borrow one of your long robes," she teased.

He looked worried. Zadir was such a romantic he once filled her bedroom with rose petals so she had to walk across a carpet of them on the floor. He probably wanted everything to be perfect even more than she did. "Don't stress about it. Sam's a film producer so she's used to juggling a lot of different things at once. It'll be fine."

"I'm sure you're right." He shoved a hand through his dark hair.

"See? Now I'm reassuring you."

He kissed her again, this time with a cheeky amount of tongue that made heat flash inside her. When he pulled back her heart was pounding.

He smiled. "Perhaps we should go see to our guests. Maybe your parents are already here and getting along like a house on fire?"

Anxiety raced through her at the thought. "A house on fire is exactly the kind of imagery I'd prefer to avoid. Let's go."

2

Royal brothers Osman, Zadir and Amahd formed a sort of receiving line in the main entrance arch that afternoon, along with the two brides, so they could greet their arriving guests. Amahd envied his older brothers their easy manner and broad circle of friends. For himself he'd be far happier tucked quietly away in his office analyzing exploration data from their newest oilfield.

"The pleasure is all mine!" Another overdressed woman with fake eyelashes flirted outrageously with him. Why would anyone wear fake eyelashes?

"Amahd, I think she liked you." His brother Zadir ribbed him after she'd sashayed off on ridiculously high heels. "She's a supermodel these days."

"A woman is most beautiful when she is modest." He spoke primly, partly knowing it would amuse his brothers to tease him, and partly because it was true. "All this makeup and tight clothing does me the favor of letting me know that the woman wearing it is not the one for me."

"You're traditionalism is admirable." Osman said it as if he was serious, but Amahd knew better. Both of his brothers had recently chosen wives who were not only foreign—Americans, no less!—but were glamorous, forceful and opinionated women with high powered careers. Clearly tradition was not foremost in their minds when choosing their brides. "But I have a feeling you're going to be single forever unless we find you a woman."

"I agree." Zadir raised a brow. "For one thing, you're always working. How are you ever going to meet someone?"

"There are certainly plenty of lovely and suitable women here tonight." His sister-in-law Sam smiled at him. He felt patronized and annoyed. Though he had to admit she looked beautiful in the deep rose colored Ubarite dress she wore, with her long, dark hair in a sleek bun. "I'm sure we could find someone to introduce you to."

"No need. I'll be fine." He must have shaken hands with two hundred people in the last three hours. He couldn't wait to sneak off and find some peace and quiet. "You concentrate on enjoying your wedding."

"Have you ever fallen in love, Amahd?" His sister in law Veronica—everyone called her Ronnie—appeared from the crowd with a glass of punch for her almost-husband Zadir. He had to admit that she also looked lovely in a crisp white dress that contrasted prettily with her smooth dark skin, and an elegant diamond clip sparkling in her short hair. Still, these bold American girls weren't for him.

"Never." The few foolish "relationships" he'd indulged in while stranded overseas for years had left him determined to hold out for the perfect woman.

"I'm sure you've broken some hearts," Ronnie continued, taking a sip of her own punch. "You're dangerously handsome."

"What nonsense. I'm glad to be of sound mind and body and that's all that matters to me." He was beginning to sound grouchy, which always amused his brothers. If only they'd all leave him alone! "I have no interest in toying with the affections of women."

"Very sensible of you." Ronnie patted his arm. "And thoughtful, too. A lot of men don't even think about the woman's feelings."

Amahd harrumphed. More condescending sympathy. It was irritating that both of his brothers had suddenly found the woman of their dreams, so now all eyes were on him. They stood to claim their titles as king after their weddings tomorrow. Like them, he couldn't become king until after he married, so there was considerable pressure on him to take a wife.

"Do any of you know who that redhead is?" Sam pointed at a woman, standing alone next to a column. A sprig of holly had caught in her bright hair and she was trying to pry it loose, which made a long strand come loose and fall across her face. She glanced around awkwardly, apparently hoping no one had noticed, as she tucked it back in.

They all shrugged. Amahd didn't remember her coming down their receiving line, but there had been so many people he'd probably just forgotten her. She was pretty, if you liked redheads.

"She looks so lost. Let me go talk to her." Sam hurried over, and soon the girl was chatting and smiling. The in-flow of guests had slowed considerably as the night drew on.

Amahd cleared his throat. "Would any of you object if I called it a night? I have some figures to go over before and I—"

"Figures to go over?" Zadir shoved him playfully. "All these beautiful women here tonight, and you want to hunker down with a spreadsheet? You're a hopeless case, brother."

"Some of us are trying to bring Ubar into the twenty-first century."

"We all are," Osman cut in. "But it doesn't have to happen in the first year. Slow and steady will get us there just fine."

Sam now headed toward them with the redhead in tow. The cheery smile plastered on Sam's face, and the way she was staring right at him, made Amahd want to run for cover.

"Amahd! Come meet Mackenzie. She's from Texas and just arrived here this afternoon. They're trying to get some dancing started on the dance floor, but everyone's too shy. Would you two do us a huge favor and go dance for a few minutes, just to get things going?

Amahd wanted to scowl at her. He was probably the last person on earth you should ask to "get things going" on a dance floor. Still, he prided himself on being a gentleman. He stuck out his hand and the redhead shook it firmly and with a warm smile.

"Nice to meet you." She looked as embarrassed by Sam's request as he did.

Still, at least it would get him away from his brothers. They were both watching him like hawks, probably wondering if this strange American woman might be his future wife. What a concept!

"I'm very pleased to meet you," he murmured. "And I suppose it would be helpful if we did as Samantha suggested."

The redhead nodded. What was her name again?

Never mind. He'd have forgotten all about her tomorrow. He simply had to gyrate on the dance floor with her for a few minutes and then he could slip away. His brothers would be none the wiser and he'd be out of this mess until the ceremony tomorrow morning.

It was awkward trying to usher her through the crowd without touching her, since naturally—as a gentleman—he wanted the woman to go first, but she didn't know the way. Eventually he was obliged to cup her elbow gently with his hand, which sent an unpleasant surge of heat right up his arm.

The silky fabric of her black dress clung to curves that were just a little too full and eye-catching to be on display. He was taller than her, so he got a disconcerting eyeful of cleavage every time he glanced at her.

Really, what was Sam thinking? What if some traditional and modest Ubarite woman was to see him right now, leading this strange American with her flame colored hair and buxom body, as if they were a couple?

He'd have to get this over with as quickly as possible.

The dance floor was in the garden, where a wood-parquet floor had been laid out under the date palms, and a band played soft music. The musicians had tried several different styles but still the dance floor was empty.

"What kind of music do you like?" he asked her.

"I like country." She smiled. His heart sank. Musicians from Ubar probably didn't even know what country music was. Sam had been drilling them on a million Christmas carols and holiday tunes until

13

they could barely remember their own names. Still, he asked the bandleader if he could play a country tune and the older man nodded enthusiastically.

Amahd led her out onto the floor, painfully aware of all the eyes on both of them, as the band struck up their tune. His heart sank when he recognized the song: *Stand by Your Man*. Many of the oilfield workers here in Ubar were from Texas, Oklahoma, etc., and loved country music, so he'd been subjected to a lot of it while out in the field.

A big grin spread across the redhead's face. She had freckles across the bridge of her nose. "It's an oldie, but a goodie."

"I suppose so." He attempted to sway to the music in a reasonably dignified manner.

Other couples followed suit and wandered onto the dance floor. To his horror they all put their arms around their partner. Apparently this was a "slow song." He shuffled forward and took one of her hands, then put the other around her waist. He didn't want to appear overly standoffish, as that would be rude.

Frankly, she looked as embarrassed as he did, which was to her credit. "Did you fly in this afternoon?" he asked, in a lame attempt to make polite conversation.

"Uh, yes, I did. What a beautiful country."

My, this was awkward. Especially since her hand was growing hot in his and he was getting very warm inside his robe. Her breasts bounced and jiggled alarmingly close to his chest and although he wanted to be appalled he felt himself growing aroused.

He glanced around him, looking everywhere for a distraction. If he could just make it through this song, he could take off.

"Do you live here?" She had full, rather red lips. He couldn't tell if she was wearing lipstick but he thought they might be natural. They contrasted with her pale, freckled skin and her amber hair. That one loose strand was now tumbling over her face again and she tried to dislodge it with a breath of air from her pursed lips.

He cursed the surge of heat that shot through his groin. Wait, she'd asked a question! What was it? "Uh, not here in the palace, no. I live a few miles away." He sounded like an idiot. "How about you?"

"I'm from a small town outside Abilene, originally, but I've been living in Midland the last few years." Her lashes were pale, and fringed greenish-hazel eyes.

"Oh." His temperature seemed to rise with every passing second. His hand on her hip sent disturbing messages to his brain about how it would like to slide a little lower and explore the full curve of her backside. He told it to mind its own business and stay just where it was.

"And show the woooorld you love him…." This song seemed to go on forever. Amahd hoped his growing arousal would be hidden by his thick sash and the dagger tucked in it. This woman was having a very disturbing effect on him. He really should get married and settle down soon. He hadn't dated anyone in a long time—too busy—and apparently he'd developed some pent-up needs.

A dimple appeared in her right cheek. "It was sweet of them to ask me to the wedding."

"Oh, yes. Of course. You're most welcome." He had absolutely no idea who had invited her to the wedding, since none of his brothers or their almost-wives recognized her. But it didn't matter. As long as he could get away from her with both of their dignity still intact he could forget he ever met her.

She swayed her hips side to side in time to the music. He wished she'd stop doing that. It was distracting and made her breasts shift inside her flimsy camisole top. He couldn't wait to get away from her before she accidentally brushed against him.

Finally, to his immense relief, the song wound to a close and he managed to disengage himself from her. "Well, we did our job." He was already backing away.

"Yes, the dance floor is full now." Couples crowded around them, jostling him as he attempted to retreat through them. "Thank you for the dance." She flashed a pretty smile.

"No, thank you." This wasn't very polite of him, but the truth was he had an erection to hide and he needed to get out of here. For the first time he truly appreciated the modesty of Ubarite dress and the way it shrouded a woman from head to toe. Not that many women in Ubar were full figured like this one, anyway.

She stood staring after him, a half smile on that lush red mouth, as he beat his retreat and headed for the far side of the garden, where he could slink down a quiet colonnade toward the room his brothers had insisted he stay in for the night.

He'd done his duty. It hadn't been easy, but he'd done it. And he'd realized it was time to put some serious effort into finding his future wife.

3

Ronnie tried to stretch her back without anyone seeing. She wasn't used to standing in high heels for so long, but Sam had rightly pointed out that a receiving line was the only sensible way to greet this many new arrivals. Guests still trickled in through the grand archway, but their numbers were thinning and the staff wheeling their impressive amounts of luggage had relaxed and started to laugh and talk amongst themselves. Everyone was getting into a party mood.

Her fiancé seemed tireless as he greeted everyone from old friends to total strangers with the same easy warmth. Unflappable and outgoing, Zadir embodied all the social skills she lacked. It was hard to believe he'd fallen so hard in love with her at their first meeting that he'd paid sixty thousand dollars at a charity auction to see her again.

Sam rushed toward her, making a T-sign with her fingers. "Time out! Fancy an escape?"

"Definitely." This was their signal to retreat to Sam's comfortable office, where they could indulge in girl-talk without shocking the servants. They walked quickly down the corridor, smiling at the guests but hoping no one waylaid them.

Sam closed the door and they collapsed into the stylish modern chairs. "Ronnie, am I overdoing it? Someone just called me a Christmas-zilla."

Ronnie laughed. "They probably didn't want to call you a bridezilla."

"I freely admit that I'm guilty of that. I guess I didn't realize how much it would mean to me to get all dressed up in a white poufy dress and say, 'I do.'"

"I know how you feel. I never really thought about getting married, but now that I am, I realized I have a lot of expectations. I don't know what I'll do if my dad doesn't show up to give me away."

"He's still not here yet?"

"I haven't seen him. My mom either. I'm worried that they ran into each other at the airport and World War Three has broken out. I've tried calling them both, but got no answer."

"You know what cell service is like here. Don't worry. They'll make it."

"But the wedding is tomorrow. What if they don't? And what about our dresses? When are we going to try them on? What if they don't fit?"

"Oh my gosh." Sam's face blanched. "I forgot all about the dresses." She pulled her phone from her pocket and dialed a number. "I hope I can get hold of them this late." She spoke slowly in the local dialect, and repeated herself a couple of times before she finally nodded. "Okay, tomorrow. First thing." Still spoken in the Ubarite dialect, those were the only words Veronica understood.

"They're not ready?"

"Something about the fabric not arriving until yesterday. The whole workshop is going to be working on them all night. At least Zadir and Osman have tuxes already,"

They'd decided to get married in western dress, rather than the multicolor sparkle-fest of Ubarite costume, partly because that's how they'd imagined their weddings since they were little. They'd forgone the traditional bridesmaids and maids of honor though. That seemed way too hard to organize with everyone coming from abroad. "I should check on the flowers."

Ronnie wanted to help. "Why don't you give me the number and I'll do that?"

"Don't worry about it. They know me so it'll be easier if I just call." Sam was already punching the numbers into her phone. Ronnie had noticed that she was rather a control freak. Probably it came from producing small budget productions where she was expected to do everything, but it made Ronnie feel like she wasn't pulling her weight.

She should be surprised that anyone answered their phone at this hour—it was already dark—but almost everyone in Ubar was at least somewhat involved in the big royal wedding celebration happening tomorrow. After talking for a few minutes in the local language, Sam hung up, shaking her head. "Why is it that if you can order forty different varieties of roses, but if you want a poinsettia, you have to order it from abroad?"

Ronnie shrugged. "I'm happy with roses."

"They're not very Christmassy. Heck, they're not at all Christmassy. At least the holly I ordered from France finally showed up, but the staff can't figure out what to do with it. The poor girl trying to arrange it in vases kept pricking herself."

Ronnie lifted a brow. "You are a Christmas-zilla."

"Only a little. And the greenery does look so pretty everywhere."

"Zadir kisses me every time we walk under mistletoe."

"Soon it'll be impossible to walk anywhere without going under mistletoe. I have a feeling we're going to have to resort to weed killer after this is over."

"No way! The butterflies are so pretty."

"True. I never thought I'd associate butterflies with Christmas, but now I don't think it will ever feel like Christmas without them."

"They're an unexpected surprise. Kind of like meeting and marrying a man from Ubar."

"Or a king from Ubar." Sam laughed. "Though if I had any idea what I was in for I might have run a mile. I can't get through a single day lately without someone asking me if I'm pregnant. All Osman's relatives are eyeing my belly and muttering to each other. You'd think my only role in life was to provide a royal heir."

"Don't worry, it will happen."

"And now my mom is here, bursting with her own pregnancy. Can you believe it? I bet she did artificial insemination, though she'd never admit it. I love her but she's completely crazy."

"You turned out sane so I'm sure the new little one will as well. Zadir and I are hoping for some good news soon, too." She smiled nervously. They'd stopped using contraception a few weeks ago, even though they weren't quite married yet.

Of course she had nothing to report yet either. "Maybe getting pregnant isn't as easy as it seems."

"Unless you're desperate not to." Sam sighed.

"Isn't that how it always works? Still, for some

reason I thought it would happen right away."

"Me too," Sam admitted. "It's humbling to have to let nature take its course. In the meantime I'm trying to control everything else with an iron fist." She poured them glasses of juice from the fridge. "So here's to us being Bride-zillas and Christmas-zillas until we have something else to obsess about."

Ronnie clinked her glass against Sam's. "It's pretty awesome that I have a sister now."

"I thought you were an only child, like me?"

"I'm talking about you, silly." It was a big admission that she felt so close to Sam. Ronnie didn't often share her feelings, but Sam deserved to know how much she appreciated her.

Sam's mouth fell open. Then snapped shut. Her deep blue eyes filled with tears.

Ronnie gulped. Had she said the wrong thing? "I meant it in a good way. I've never had a friend I could be so blunt with before."

"Me either." She leaned forward and gave Ronnie a hug.

A knock on the door startled them both.

"Come in," they called in unison.

A frightened looking male servant peered around the door and stammered in the local dialect. "Miss Veronica, there's someone here to see you."

Ronnie gasped. "My mom!" Then she frowned. "Or my dad." She gulped. "Or both. I'd better go."

4

"How's my princess?" Ronnie's dad kissed her on both cheeks, and her chest filled with joy.

"You made it!" She'd been growing increasingly nervous since it got dark.

"Did you think I wouldn't?" As always, he wore a long cashmere coat over a grey suit. "I'd never miss my little girl's wedding. You remember Anushka?"

"Of course." She hoped she wasn't expected to kiss her "mother-in-law", who was one year her junior, on her rosy cheek. "Nice to see you again." They shook hands. Really, she had nothing against this woman, though she knew her mom was unlikely to feel the same way.

"Anushka's pregnant!" Her dad's smile shone in his dark complexion. "Isn't that great?"

"Wow. Yes. That is exciting." Panic clutched her gut. Would this baby be her sister? So far her father had resisted all his wives' attempts to get him to reproduce, so in fact it would be her only sister. "Let's celebrate. I'll go get us some punch."

It was a relief to duck away. She needed a moment. Now her mom was really going to go ballistic. She'd tried many times to convince her dad to give Ronnie a sister, and he'd steadfastly refused.

Ronnie retrieved three glasses from the punch bowl station, and hurried back. "When are you due?"

"Six weeks." Anushka had a deep, sultry voice with an Eastern European accent. "Though you'd never know it to look at me." She waved a ringed hand over her still-svelte body. Her giant bust threw everything else into shadow. "Shapewear. I'm going to bring out a line of it next year."

"Wow. That's great." Ronnie blinked.

"Anushka is a hand model," added her dad. "She's been able to work right through the pregnancy. She uses herbs to prevent water retention."

"Maybe you'll be able to give me some tips when I decide to have a baby." Ronnie wasn't going to admit to anyone but Sam that she was already trying. Apparently everyone here was blossoming with life, except the brides.

"Oh, you must definitely have a baby." Anushka swatted a butterfly off her glass. "If you like I could teach you some really cool tricks for your wedding night. To make sure the little sperms can swim all the way up to your egg."

"Uh." Ronnie stared, unable to form words. "Maybe later." Out of the corner of her eye, she saw a giant rolling cart piled high with Louis Vuitton luggage.

Her mom.

Sam hurried along the corridor, anxious to tell people that the buffet dinner was being served in the main dining room. They'd decided to abandon the usual "rehearsal dinner" since people were arriving from all different time zones and would be hungry at different times. The servants had already been through making announcements, but their English was experimental at best and she couldn't be sure anyone would understand them.

As she knocked on the door to one friend's room, the hallway lights went out. Flaming torches on the wall kept her from being plunged into total darkness. A shriek echoed along the hallway.

Uh-oh. She pulled out her phone and called the maintenance manager. Who didn't answer his phone. She called Osman. "Sweetie, I hate to bother you, but do you know what's going on with the lights?"

She could hear Osman speaking rapidly to someone in the local language. She'd been studying it for months now but it was so complicated and seemed to be composed of about twenty other languages—none of which she knew—so learning it would be a lifetime's work.

"The power's gone down."

"I can see that." They lost power several times a week. Usually the event was invisible. "What about the backup generators?"

"They've run out of fuel. Iskar forgot that we'd have lights blazing all through the palace. They've sucked every drop from the tanks."

"And I don't suppose he'll be able to buy more at this time of night." Ubar ground to a standstill at dusk. "I guess I should have ordered flashlights for everyone."

"Don't worry, my love. Ubar has been lit by flaming torches for thousands of years."

"I know, but our guests aren't used to that. And I told Iskar not to light the torches in the guest rooms because they're a fire hazard when people aren't careful."

Guests emerged from the dark rooms, tripping over their eveningwear and stumbling into the flickering half-light of the hallway.

"We'll manage. It'll be more romantic this way."

She let out a breath. Osman never let the "small stuff" get to him. Of course her job was to sweat the small stuff so it didn't turn into big stuff, but this time she planned to listen to his advice. "You're right." Guests crowded around her. She couldn't remember even half of their names. "I'll bring everyone down to the dining room so we can enjoy a candlelit dinner."

"Mom!" Ronnie rushed toward her mother. Who vanished as darkness descended on the main hallway. It took a few moments for her eyes to adjust enough for her to pick her way through the crowds. "Mom, where are you?"

"I'm here, darling."

Her mom's deep, raspy voice filled her with emotion and she was glad the darkness hid the tears filling her eyes. "Oh my goodness, you have no idea how glad I am that you're here."

"Nothing on earth would make me miss my baby's wedding." Her mom hugged her to her ample bosom and Ronnie drew in her mom's familiar scent of Chanel #5 and gourmet chocolates.

"Why have we been plunged into darkness? Is the curtain about to go up?" Her mom saw the whole world in stage terms, even though she hadn't been on one in decades. As usual she was dressed like a diva in satin and sequins. She refused to own a single item of clothing that didn't sparkle.

Ronnie laughed. "No. The electricity has probably been overwhelmed by the celebration. Come in and let's find you a glass of champagne. The staff will know what to do with your bags." The sudden darkness was a stroke of luck. Now her mom wouldn't be able to see Ronnie's father unless he came right over to her. If she could get her mom settled in and relaxed, things were far more likely to go well.

"Thank God you were sensible enough not to ask your father! I still can't believe he married a woman younger than his own daughter. That should be illegal."

"Uh." Ronnie's heart crumpled in her chest. It's not like she could keep her dad a secret forever. He was going to give her away tomorrow. Still, her mom had only just arrived. No need to upset her already. "Let's go get your hands hennaed! It's an Ubarite tradition that all the women at a wedding get decorated." Her dad's hand-model wife was unlikely to be there, since henna took weeks to fade completely away. "We can do it together. It'll be fun."

"Shouldn't I at least find my room and—"

"No, don't worry about that. I'll take you there later. You're in the room right next to mine and there's probably chaos in the corridor as the servants go around with lanterns. Much better to stay out of their way."

"If you say so, baby. It certainly is wonderful to see you, even if I can't really see you right now." Ronnie held fast to her mom's hand as they wove through the knots of people. Her eyes adjusted to the flickering lights from the torches on the walls, which were the only light source on a normal night. She led her into the comfortable sitting room, where three girls were painting the female guests' hands with intricate patterns.

"Where's that handsome husband of yours? Are you sure he's not going to break your heart?" Her mom looked up from having her palm painted with tiny swirls. "I'm very suspicious of a man who's that good looking."

"That was exactly my reaction when I first met him. I thought he seemed like trouble." Ronnie grinned. "But he has me convinced that he's madly in love with me and will cherish me forever."

Her mom sighed. "That's what I thought, once upon a time, before your dad destroyed my faith in men."

"Mom, all men are different. I've learned that I have to give him the benefit of the doubt. I can't make assumptions about men based on someone completely different."

"I suppose you're right. I just don't want my baby to get her heart broken the way mine was."

Ronnie was touched by her mom's affectionate worry. They'd grown distant and impatient with each other in recent years: Ronnie exasperated that her mom rarely got out of bed, and her mom annoyed that Ronnie was too busy to hover about her bedside lamenting with her. A recent heart-trouble scare had made Ronnie realize how much her mom really meant to her. "I can handle it, Mom. You raised me to be tough on the inside. I honestly never thought I'd be crazy enough to fall in love, but I have and it's wonderful."

Her mom's big, mournful eyes glittered with sudden tears. "I'd love to squeeze your hand now, sweetie, but I'm afraid these lovely ladies will never forgive me." She smiled at the girls putting the finishing touches on their henna. "You enjoy this magical time. You deserve it. I feel bad that we didn't celebrate Christmas properly when you were growing up."

Ronnie sucked in a breath, trying to keep her emotions in check. Her mom had refused to make a big deal of celebrating the holiday since they "weren't a real family" any more. Her early memories of stockings stuffed with presents and her dad pretending to be Santa had been replaced with memories of gift cards purchased by the maid. Her mom had steadfastly refused to fill their apartment with the scent of a real tree because, "it's too depressing when it dies."

They'd celebrated one way, though. "You did always play Bing Crosby's White Christmas."

"And Ella Fitzgerald's." Her mom beamed. "I brought them with me on my iPhone. We can listen to them later when we're alone."

Ronnie sighed. Her mom being here felt like the Christmas present she'd never dared hope for. "I'd love that."

Their hands finished, they headed out into the garden, where lanterns lit the night and soft music filled the air. Ronnie introduced her mom to Sam and Osman, who took them to meet a friend of his who'd just arrived from France. Dressed in a dark suit and a rich burgundy and gold tie, the older man bowed low when introduced to Ronnie's mom.

"Selena Wilmington." He spoke with a French accent. "I saw you perform at the Café de Paris in London on September 23, 1988. It's a night I shall never forget."

Ronnie stared at her mom, whose smile spread

across her face as he kissed her hand like a gallant knight. "I can't believe you can even recognize me."

"You're even more radiant now than you were then." He was a handsome man in his fifties, dapper and elegant.

"Nonsense! My daughter hasn't even let me go to my room to freshen up yet."

"You are fresh as the mistletoe my friend's lovely new bride has garlanded the place with." Ronnie's mom burst out laughing. Ronnie cast a glance at Sam, who looked back in surprise. "Would you do me the honor of dancing with me?"

"Why, I'd be delighted."

Ronnie watched in amazement as her mom, who probably hadn't danced in twenty years, took his hand and let him lead her to an open space where couples swayed to the soft music.

"Am I dreaming?" Ronnie clutched Sam's arm. "Because I don't want to wake up."

"Something's in the air." Sam blinked. "Something big."

Osman answered his phone, listened for a moment, then frowned. "I've got to go out for a while."

"But where?" Distress wrinkled Sam's smooth brow. "It's the eve of our wedding! Can't you forget about business at least until after our wedding night?"

Oman stroked her upper arm softly. "The power outage. Rifal has a report that it's the result of deliberate sabotage. It's important that I investigate personally."

"Is it really?" Sam's voice rose. "Isn't that what all your staff are for? And where's the famous Gibran who's supposed to come and save the day?"

They'd been talking for some time about a famous security expert who was some kind of family relative. He was awaited with all the anticipation of the Second Coming, but had yet to make an appearance.

"He'll be here when he's ready. For now the responsibility to protect our people lies with me." He spoke so tenderly that Ronnie's heart ached for him. "You know how much that means to me."

"I do," said Sam softly. "It's one of the many things I love about you."

"I'll be back as soon as I can." He kissed her on the lips and made a swift departure.

"Dammit. Things were going so well." Sam's eyes shone with tears.

"They still are, Sam." Ronnie squeezed her arm. "He'll be back soon. And maybe the lights will even come back on first." She saw a couple moving toward the dance floor, and her blood ran cold. "Oh no. My dad and his new wife."

"I thought you were thrilled that they'd arrived."

"I am. But my mom has no idea he's here."

5

Ronnie braced herself for the inevitable fireworks. "I'd better go intercept. I probably should have warned both of them, but I didn't dare." She drew in a deep breath and marched toward the dance floor.

Her dad, arms around his nubile young wife, was just noticing her mom in the semi-darkness. She watched his lips part.

Ronnie's mom—much to Ronnie's continued surprise—was swaying to the beat with Osman's friend. She realized that she should have paid closer attention to his name. Solomon? She couldn't remember the first name at all.

She hurried to her father. "Uh, dad. Would you like to go meet Osman's brothers?" Already her nerves were failing.

"Is that your mother?" He continued staring at her.

She gulped. "Yes. I didn't tell you she'd be here because I thought it might keep you from coming. It means the world to me that you're here to give me away." She almost felt like he might turn and run right now. And she couldn't really blame him when she recalled some of the scenes her mom had caused over the years.

"I'd never miss your wedding." Her dad had stopped dancing. "You're the only daughter I have."

So far. She dismissed the selfish thought. "So, you're not mad?"

"Not at all. But I suppose we'd better get the meet and greet over with." Her dad looked curiously at her mom's elegant companion. "Who is she dancing with?"

"A friend of Osman's." Her partner hadn't taken his eyes off her. He looked rapt, and weirdly enough she was gleaming with good spirits, too. "Perhaps we should wait until the music stops." She didn't want to break the spell. She hadn't seen her mom look this happy in years.

Her dad lifted a brow. "You're afraid of her. Let's get this over with." He walked up to her and tapped her on the arm. She turned, but instead of the pantomime expression of distress and horror that Ronnie had anticipated, she smiled. "Oh, hello Victor. This is Tislat Suleiman, an old friend from my singing days."

Her dance partner shook her dad's hand and Ronnie's mom continued to glow like a star on opening night as her dad introduced Anushka. They didn't shake hands—which would have made Ronnie very nervous—but simply nodded their greetings politely, then went back to dancing.

Ronnie pinched herself. It hurt, which meant this was really happening. Zadir moved up beside her and whispered in her ear. "See? I told you everything would work out fine."

"I'm nervous that it's the calm before the storm." This didn't feel right.

"Just relax and enjoy it."

"Easier said than done."

"Dance with me." Already his hand was on her waist and he tugged her into the middle of the floor.

"What? Right now?" There were still guests from the States that she hadn't greeted yet.

"Yes, right now." His blue gaze dared her to defy him, and his arms around her waist added to the challenge.

"Don't you have things to do?" Desire flared inside her as her body bumped against his. The music had slowed to a romantic, jazzy number.

"The only thing I need to do right now is dance with my beautiful wife."

"Almost-wife," she corrected.

"Same thing." His slow smile was contagious—she felt it creep across her mouth as her arms rose around his neck. "All I know is that you're mine."

"Not yet. I could change my mind before tomorrow morning," she teased. It was infuriating how Zadir was always so sure of himself. He never seemed to seriously consider that they wouldn't end up together, just because that's what he wanted.

"Then I'd better make sure you think of nothing all night but how much you want to marry me." He twirled her around, dipping her slightly, which made her gasp.

"Shouldn't we spend the night apart? It's tradition."

"Perish the thought." He stepped forward, pushing her thigh back with his. Arousal sizzled through her. How did he always have this effect on her? Common sense flew out the window when she was around Zadir. "Some traditions are worth keeping. Others are foolish habits that are best discarded."

His fingertips pressed gently into the area right above her behind. They strayed a little lower and her skin sizzled through her thin evening gown. He whirled them through the crowd as excitement flashed over her. She'd thought her life was pretty exciting before she met him—she was busy with architecture clients, travel and new commissions—but Zadir had swept her into a whole other world.

He kissed her, his lips meeting hers exactly at the moment that the saxophone launched into a haunting solo. He hugged her to him and she could almost feel their hearts beating against each other. For once she was wearing such high heels that she could look him right in the eye. "You're a very persistent man, Zadir Al Kilanjar."

"I know what I want." A smile flashed in his blue eyes, though his expression was serious. "And I want you in bed, right now."

She tried to ignore the surge of heat that rose through her. "That would be rude. We're the hosts."

"Our guests will be fine without us." His low voice crept into her ear as he dipped her again, then pulled her even closer. "I, however, am developing a...*situation*...that only you can fix."

She could feel it beneath the sash of his robe, jutting against her belly. A giggle rose inside her. "So you are. That is a problem."

"With only one solution."

"A cold shower."

"Or some hot loving." He spoke so low that no one but her could hear him. His breath, hot on her cheek, excited her, and his rich masculine scent tormented her senses.

"Let's go." Suddenly she couldn't wait either. She glanced back toward her mother—still happily dancing—and her father—fussing over Anushka—then fixed her eyes on the door. If they could just make it out of here without being waylaid, they could be alone behind closed doors in less than two minutes.

"Why do you have to be so beautiful?" Zadir's rough voice in her ear made her smile.

"Me? Have you noticed all the gorgeous women here tonight?"

"I'm only interested in one woman." He led her by the hand across the dance floor, under a row of palms, and back toward the main hallway that led toward the bedrooms. "The others are irrelevant to me."

Ronnie faltered as one of the staff started toward them with a questioning look on his face. He looked like he was about to ask whether to open another crate of champagne or bake another batch of pastries.

But the urgency of their movements and the intent look on their faces must have scared him off, as he stepped aside and hurried off in another direction. "Narrow escape," she whispered.

"Thank heaven. I can't wait." His voice was gruff with urgency. "I need to get that gorgeous dress off your gorgeous body before I lose my mind."

They almost ran along the hallway, her heels clicking on the mosaic-tiled floor. Desire heated her skin and quickened her breathing. Light from the flickering torches along the wall cast tall shadows around them.

"I hope nobody saw us sneak off." She glanced back. Music followed them, growing fainter, as they hurried for their room.

"I don't care what they saw." Zadir's eyes flashed. "A man should be able to make love to his own wife."

"Almost-wife." They were close now, and excitement built like butterflies inside her.

Zadir pulled open the door to their room and they rushed in, slamming it behind them. Within seconds they were on the bed, clawing at each other's clothes. Zadir's traditional robe was off in a flash, pulled over his head to reveal his hard stomach and powerful chest.

The delicate buttons down the back of Ronnie's sleek designer dress took a little more work, but soon she was naked, with reflected light from the brazier dancing over her skin.

They climbed onto the mattress, kneeling in front of each other. Ronnie's skin tingled as excitement and anticipation crackled between them.

Still…. "What if this is bad luck?" This much happiness made Ronnie nervous. She wasn't used to it.

"I'll take my chances." Zadir's low voice rumbled against her skin as he placed a line of gentle kisses down her face and neck, between her breasts, and over her very sensitive belly. She had to struggle not to laugh as he blew into her belly button. Already her insides were quivering.

"You're such a tease."

"I can't help myself," he breathed. His tongue slipped between her thighs and she bucked slightly as it found its sensitive target. "Driving you wild is too much fun."

Fingers fisted in his hair, she gave herself over to

sensation as he pleasured her with the tip of his tongue. Soon, wet and ready, she couldn't take any more. "Stop, please!" She wanted him inside her.

"What is it sweetheart?" His blue eyes gleamed with mischief.

Make love to me now! She still wasn't quite uninhibited enough to demand it. "I want...." How could you put it politely?

"You want what, my love?" He cocked his head, as if curious. A dimple appeared in his left cheek. He rose and sucked first one nipple, then the next, until they stood on end, gleaming and sizzling with arousal.

Then he waited. All two hundred pounds of solid muscle, kneeling just a few superheated inches from her desperately aroused body, hard as rock ledge and with more self control than she could stand. She watched his chest rise and fall. Saw that dimple deepen.

Frustration and passion flashed through her. She drew in a shaky breath, barely able to stay upright. "I want—I need—" Words failed her and she pushed him roughly back onto the bed. His head sank into the pillows and she knew the grin on his face should infuriate her but instead it just excited her more. She climbed over him and took him inside her with a shiver of deep relief.

"Ah," he murmured. "Now I see exactly what you want."

"Stop talking," she commanded softly. She couldn't stop the smile crossing her mouth. She leaned forward to kiss him and her nipples brushed his chest. She started to move, deepening the connection between them and letting all her inhibitions melt away as pleasure rose through her.

Zadir's hands roamed over her body, and she could hear his low moans of pleasure as she guided them further into a private world of passion. Soon, he was on top, burying himself deep in her and kissing her like she was the only source of sustenance on earth.

When they finally climaxed it was so intense and explosive that she couldn't remember where they were, or why. She had no idea how long they'd been here and didn't care.

"Feeling better now, my love?"

"You're cruel." She ran a thumb over his sensual mouth.

"It's too much fun to tease you. You made me set up an entire charity auction just to go on a single date with you, remember?"

"You're never going to let me forget that, are you?" Her chest still heaved with the aftereffects of their lovemaking.

"You wanted to walk away and forget all about that night we shared in the desert."

"I was an idiot." She bit her lip. It was hard to believe that she'd been so afraid of the passion that had flared between them that she hoped to simply avoid him. "And I almost threw away our whole future."

"Lucky thing I don't take no for an answer." His eyes twinkled.

"It is." She sighed and rested her head on his chest. "I thought my life was so great traveling around designing buildings here and there. Now I'm creating a whole city here in Ubar. It's not something I could even have dared to dream of."

"Here in Ubar we believe in destiny. Ubar was

your destiny, I am your destiny. You just needed a little time to accept it." He stroked her cheek gently with his broad thumb.

"I'm the luckiest woman alive." It wasn't easy to admit it. Habitually shy and reserved, she used to keep her feelings to herself. Here in Ubar she could feel herself opening up like a flower blooming in a long-awaited rain. "I love you Zadir Al Kilanjar."

"I love you more." One dark brow lifted slightly.

"You're so competitive."

"So are you." Already his hands slid up and down her body, sparking trails of arousal.

"Don't you think we should get back to her guests?" Her belly quivered, wanting him inside her again.

He buried his face in her neck and inhaled her scent. "Definitely not."

6

A knock on the door in the dead of night made Sam sit up in her bed with a start. "Osman?"

"It is Rifal, madam." One of her husband's men.

Panic flared in her chest. Why would he disturb her at night? Was something horribly wrong? "What is it?"

"There's been a shooting." His voice traveled through the door and hit her straight in the heart like a bullet. Terror spiked through her as she flew out of bed and tugged the door open. "Is my husband okay?" All her silly fussing over the Christmas decorations and the wedding meant nothing if she didn't have Osman to share them with.

"Yes, your majesty—" The words that followed were a blur as she sagged with relief. It was hard to act with the dignity of a queen at moments like this. "And he said to go ahead with the ceremony even though he won't be back until mid morning."

"Mid morning? But Ronnie and Zadir's ceremony is at ten. What if he's not back in time?"

"He'll be here." Rifal bowed. Sam wanted to shake him for almost making her have a heart attack, and now leaving her frustrated. Not that she'd been sleeping anyway.

"Wait! Who shot who? Did they find out what's going on with the power?"

"The facility appears to have been sabotaged. Two men have been apprehended and one of them shot at the guards before he was captured. No one was hurt."

"Are there other saboteurs running around?"

"I can't say, your majesty." He bowed again.

"Thank you, Rifal." She wanted to call Osman but didn't want to disturb him if he was in the middle of a sensitive operation.

She'd just have to distract herself with the million little details of the festivities tomorrow, and making sure that Ronnie and Zadir's wedding was everything Ronnie dreamed it would be. Sam was already married by Ubarite convention, so her wedding was just for fun, but Ronnie's would be the moment where she and Zadir committed their lives to each other.

She paced anxiously around her room until dawn started to pierce through the intricate patterns on the filigreed wood shutters. When her phone rang she almost jumped out of her skin. "Osman?" She hadn't even glanced at the number.

"No darling, it's dad."

"How is your phone working here?"

"It isn't, I borrowed one from the staff. Your mother appears to be in labor."

"What?" Sam's adrenaline surged. "When is she due?"

"In two months." Her dad sounded like nothing was wrong. But then he was an actor.

"Oh my goodness. That's way too early! Let me call a doctor. Hopefully they can stop it. Are you in your room?"

"Yes dear, and the doctor is here. He's given her a

41

shot of some kind. Why don't you come on over." He said it like he was inviting her over for a barbeque, not an emergency labor intervention. But staying calm was good in a situation like this. She hoped her mom wasn't panicking, because that would only make things worse.

Sam tugged on a shirt and pants, and sprinted along the corridor to the room she'd chosen for her parents because it was the largest and most beautiful guest room with a glorious view of the orchard outside. Now she cursed herself for not picking the closest. A knot of servants had gathered outside the door, murmuring anxiously. One carried a large brass bowl, another a jug of steaming water and yet another bore a stack of white towels, like they were going to deliver the baby right here in the bedroom.

Which was, of course, exactly how they did things in Ubar.

Sam squeezed through them and burst into the room. "Mom, are you okay?"

"Yes, sweetheart. The doctor gave me a shot and it seems to have stopped the contractions." Sam drew in a grateful gasp of air, which made her realize she'd been holding her breath. Her mom had a surprised look on her face, but that could be from all the Botox and facelifts. "Would my baby need a green card if she's born in Ubar?"

Sam burst out laughing. "I don't think so. But she could certainly have dual citizenship. Are you sure it's a girl?"

"Yes." Her mom smiled. She was wearing full makeup, probably applied between contractions before calling for help. "We have an album of ultrasound photos already."

"I can't believe you didn't even tell me you were pregnant."

"Your mother didn't want a media circus," explained her father, stroking his wife's shoulder. "And we didn't want you to worry."

It's true. She would have worried. But her mom must have been pregnant even when she and Osman went to visit them in California earlier in the year. "You're a dark horse."

"Nonsense, darling, I just don't want the paparazzi trying to take pictures of me looking fat. I have a big role coming up next summer, in Hedda Gabler at the Mizner theater! I don't want them to start thinking I won't be available."

"I can keep a secret, you know." Sam was pretty mad. "And we could have prepared better for something like this." She gestured to the staff, with their towels and jugs and bowls.

"It seems you're marvelously prepared already, darling. I do love this sweet country of yours." Her mom let out a dramatic sigh. "I suppose I should try to get some rest before morning." She pulled down her blackout mask over her eyes, shutting out the world.

Sam looked at her dad. Who shrugged. At least he seemed to be taking the whole thing in stride. "All right, Dad. Let me know if anything happens again, okay? Preferably before you call in the cavalry."

Sam consulted with the doctor, and thanked the servants for responding so quickly but told them to put everything away for now and keep quiet about this. There were probably journalists at the wedding and she didn't want all the stories about it to focus on her mom's miracle pregnancy.

At eight-thirty in the morning, Osman still wasn't home. Sam gave into the urge to call him. "I miss you."

"I miss you, too, beloved. I can't wait to see you in your finery."

"You really won't be home until I'm all dressed? It'll be very last minute since the dresses are not even here yet." They should have arrived by now. Another thing to worry about.

"I'm interrogating these men we found at the power station. I have to make sure there are no further threats, especially with so many visitors in our country."

"I understand. I just wish I could hug you right now."

"I'll make up for it later. *Ilyrimas*, my love."

Sam smiled. She loved Ubarite endearments. "You carry my heart, too."

She put down her phone with a sigh. There was nothing for it but to forge ahead without him. First she needed to find out what was going on with their dresses. A shriek outside her door startled her, and she opened it to see a black and white goat trotting by.

7

Sam realized that the cry had emerged from the mouth of an older lady who was screaming not at the goat but at the sight of a young man, dagger raised, charging after it. "Don't kill that beautiful creature!"

"Aunt Edna, you're up early." Sam recognized her mother's sister, who—like Sam's mom—had grown up on a farm in the Midwest and run as far away from it as possible.

"You have to stop him!"

"It's probably for the wedding feast. I'm afraid goat is a popular dish here."

"But look at it. The intelligence in its eyes makes killing it a crime."

The goat darted around a corner, with the man in hot pursuit. Aunt Edna ran after him, her colorful kaftan flopping at her heels.

Oh dear.

The sound of hooves on the mosaic tile floors made Sam turn and look in the other direction, where a pretty honey-colored goat was trotting after its friend. Sam reached out and grabbed his collar. "Whoa there. Where do you think you're going?"

Other guests had emerged from their rooms at the commotion. "You aren't really going to kill it are you?

Look how cute it is. Did you know that goats have rectangular pupils in their eyes?" People crowded around to peer into the goat's rather lovely blue eyes.

"I'll do my best to grant a reprieve. Maybe we can have chicken instead." Sam started walking along the corridor, trying to lead the goat—which proved surprisingly strong and unwilling.

"He's afraid of you." A girl came forward. Probably one of the brothers' college friends. "Here, let me." She grabbed hold of the collar. The startled goat swiftly head-butted her, knocked her off her feet, and took off running along the corridor.

"Are you okay?" Sam offered her a hand. Embarrassed, the girl—fully dressed in wedding finery—nodded and scrambled upright in her stilettoes. Sam found the goat further down the hallway, munching on some decorative mistletoe and disturbing the crowd of butterflies already claiming it. She phoned the head of staff. "Why are there goats running through the palace?"

He apologized profusely and explained that their pen had collapsed in the night and they'd all escaped. Sam attempted to explain that Americans wouldn't want to eat animals they'd formed a personal relationship with, so it was now important to serve something else.

Later she realized she probably should have specified what, but instead she hurried back to her room, anxious to get dressed so she could make sure everything was in place for the ceremony at ten.

"Deck the halls with boughs of holly…" The song suddenly blasted over the palace intercom, announcing that the power was back on. On her way

to the garden, Ronnie put a hand to her chest, trying to calm herself. Why was she so nervous? She and Zadir had been living as man and wife for some weeks now.

Maybe it was all the people. And the goats. A dark brown one darted past her with a sprig of holly in its mouth.

"'Tis the season to be jolly…" And Christmas always made her feel emotional. It was supposed to be such a happy time, when families gathered together to give thanks for the birth of their savior, but in her house it has always been a time when she was painfully aware of how different her family was from those happy ones on TV.

But today, her mother and father were gathered under the same roof, the smell of cinnamon and roasting nuts filled the air, and joyous music was now playing on everyone's nerves. She should be overcome with joy.

Instead she was about to start sobbing.

"Sweetheart, you're shaking." Zadir rubbed her shoulders, which were the only part of her not currently swathed in crystal-encrusted white fabric. At least the dress fit.

"Oh no! You're not supposed to see me until the wedding." She stared at him in horror. Surely this was terrible luck. Yes, they'd spent the night together, but she'd dressed with all-female attendants who had strict orders to keep him at bay. "You need to go away."

"What?"

"Surely you know that. You lived in the west for years."

"That I can't look at my lovely bride on her

wedding day?" He wasn't listening at all. He moved in front of her and took her hands in his. "What foolishness is that?"

"It's so you can be surprised when you see me coming down the aisle." She blinked, taking in the sight of him in a sleek black tux, blue eyes gleaming with excitement. She started to relax. "But it's okay. I forgive you. And I'm sorry for snapping. I'm just jumpy."

"I forgive you, too. For anything and everything. For ever." He swooped in and planted a firm kiss on her mouth. As his tongue darted between her lips, her nerves evaporated.

"Why do you always make me feel so much better about everything?" she murmured, when their lips finally parted.

"Because I'm your soul mate and life partner, here to strew your path with roses. How long until we're officially hitched?"

Ronnie pulled her phone out of the pocket concealed in her voluminous skirt and checked the time. "About twenty minutes. If I can manage not to die of fright before then."

"I don't care about your old western superstitions. I'm not letting you out of my sight for a moment."

"Don we now our gay apparel…." How could the same song still be playing? Time was moving so slowly Ronnie thought she might go out of her mind.

"Okay."

Sam felt really strange getting dressed when Osman wasn't even back yet. She'd tried calling again but he didn't answer. She refused to even contemplate that anything bad had happened.

Besides, in that case someone would call her.

Wouldn't they?

Her dress hung on the bed frame, still in the bag from the dressmaker. She hadn't even dared look at it because it was too late to make changes now.

She dabbed pale gold eye shadow on her eyelid and started to apply eyeliner. She wasn't very good with makeup, but it did make people look better in pictures and she wanted the photos to be memorable.

Festive music rang through the palace, and she could hear the happy shrieks of children. She'd insisted that all the staff bring their children today, and she had gifts for everyone. She'd always hated how children often weren't welcome at weddings, and had always vowed to include them, even if that made things a little noisier.

She couldn't wait to have her own children. Osman would be such a wonderful father, and it would be nice for him to have the chance to create the happy family he never got to enjoy.

A knock on the door made her smudge the eyeliner. "Osman!" Her heart leapt.

"I'm sorry. It's just me." Ronnie peeked around the door. "My dress fits." Her dress was stunning. With her hair in a lovely updo, decorated with little white flowers, she looked so radiant that Sam wanted to cry.

"Don't cry!" Ronnie rushed toward her. "You'll smudge your makeup. Here, let me finish that." She expertly drew a line above Sam's lashes. "How does your dress look?"

"I haven't dared find out." She glanced at the hanger. "I suppose it's now or never."

Ronnie retrieved the hanger while Sam put in

some delicate pearl earrings that her grandmother had worn on her wedding day. Outside the bag the dress looked foolishly ornate and fluffy, like something the girl on top of a cake would wear.

"Put it on," scolded Ronnie gently. "Osman will be here any second."

"He'll need to get dressed, too."

"You know he can do pretty much anything in thirty seconds. He's infuriatingly capable." Ronnie winked.

"Not everything," said Sam with a sly smile. "Some things take at least a few minutes. But now you've distracted me. Let me get this on."

She poked her toes carefully into the pool of white tulle and Ronnie helped her lift the bodice up to her chest. "Goodness, it's heavier than I expected."

"All the seed beads. They're so lovely. They must have taken hours to sew." Beads of ice white, pale ivory and frosty silver swirled in a beautiful pattern that covered the bodice and dripped down onto the full skirt. Sam pulled the bodice up over her breasts and Ronnie went behind her to zip it up.

Sam felt Ronnie tug gingerly up to her waist, then stop.

"What's wrong?"

"Hmm. There's a big gap. Let me pull the two sides together a bit." Sam felt her yank on them, then tug again at the zipper. "I think we need a third pair of hands."

"It won't close?" Sam felt tears welling in her eyes. Why hadn't she been more efficient about getting the dresses made earlier?

"It might, if we can find a vice grip, or a pair of hands just like one."

"Oh no." Sam tried to suck in her waistline. "I must have gained weight. Which is weird. Usually I drop weight if I'm nervous and busy."

"Don't worry. We'll get it closed. I have a lot of experience from getting my bags zipped each time I headed off to boarding school. Usually I would just sit on them and keep yanking, but in this case—"

Another knock on the door made them both turn. Sam shrieked with relief and joy to see her big handsome husband standing there. Her eyes filled with tears again. "I can't get my dress done up."

Osman crossed the room in two strides and laid a reassuring kiss on her lips that reduced her blood pressure by a good ten points. Within seconds he'd lined up both sides of the dress and held them steady while Ronnie raised the zipper up to the top and let out a whoop of victory. "Just don't breathe for a few hours, okay?"

"Okay. I can't breathe anyway with so much going on. Did I smudge my makeup?"

"You look stunning." Osman's deep voice soothed her. The way he looked at her she really did feel radiant and beautiful. "Now I'd better take a quick shower and throw something on myself. Do you think people will be offended if I wear pajamas?" Mischief twinkled in his eyes.

"I doubt anyone but the servants would even notice. One long man-robe looks the same as another to most of our guests," said Sam with a smile. "But Rifal brought this for you." She pointed to a sleek black tux, hung over a snowy white shirt. "We're going western today, remember?"

"Of course, I'd completely forgotten." He hurried into the bathroom to take a shower. Once the water was running he turned and called back. "But I'm most looking forward to the part where I get to take it off."

8

Sam watched as Ronnie's dad walked her proudly down the aisle, and she couldn't stop her lip from quivering as she watched Ronnie and Zadir repeat their vows. They sat outside in the garden, under the shade of the orchard trees, in rows of chairs arranged on either side of a makeshift aisle strewn with rose petals.

Zadir went first, ridiculously handsome in his black tux, crisp against a white shirt and tie.

"I promise to share my life with you as both a lover and a friend. I vow to nurture and support your dreams and help you to achieve your goals. I promise to cherish and love you, through any adversity that comes our way, and to grow with you as we build our family and share our lives."

He slipped the ring onto her finger, eyes shining with emotion. "I love you, Ronnie, and I'm so overjoyed that you agreed to be my wife."

Ronnie looked so beautiful in her delicate white dress, with tiny flowers glowing in her dark hair. "I promise to share life's challenges and joys at your side. I promise to be your partner in parenthood, your ally in conflict, and your companion in adventure. I promise to be your greatest fan and your toughest critic and to love you each and every day that we're blessed to spend together."

She slid the ring onto his finger, and a murmur of appreciation spread through the crowds. "I love you Zadir, and I'm thrilled that you are daring enough to be my husband."

Sam became so overwhelmed with emotion that she actually let out a little whimper.

A couple of people sitting nearby turned to look at her, probably wondering if she was okay. Was she? She was probably just overtired and frazzled from all the organizing and decorating, and spending the night before the ceremony without her beloved husband. It was all a bit much, apparently.

Ronnie and Zadir kissed, and the crowd clapped and whistled. They were the cutest couple. Ronnie had blossomed in the months since she'd moved here, shedding much of her reserve and becoming— as she'd said herself—the closest thing Sam ever had to a sister.

Sam herself had moved here—a land where she didn't speak the language and knew only one person and his family—with no idea whether she'd ever even have a friend again. And now she had a brilliant, funny and sweet girlfriend to share all their new experiences. It would have been far too much to ever ask for and she didn't take it for granted.

She dabbed quickly at a tear running down her cheek. She had her own ceremony to get through next, and she wasn't sure how she'd manage without bawling.

"Are you okay?" Ronnie rushed up to her.

"I'm feeling very emotional. I suppose that's normal on your wedding day. Or is it? I am already married to him after all. I almost wish we could skip this big do I've been planning for so long and I could just hold him and have a good cry."

"You're probably overwhelmed by the excitement of having so many visitors and all our family members gathered together for the first time. It's wonderful, but it's also rather emotionally draining."

"I suppose you're right. My mom's labor scare wasn't the ideal way to start the day."

Ronnie nodded sympathetically. Zadir strode up to his new wife and kissed her. "How are you, Mrs. Al Kilanjar?"

"Wonderful," she said, smiling. "And you?"

"You do realize that's not your real title."

"I suppose it is kind of western. What should I call myself?"

He pretended to frown. "According to our convention, your mother's name would be in there. Her name is Selena, so I think it would be something like, "Her Glorious Majesty Veronica bin Selena Al Kilanjar."

Veronica grinned. "It has a nice ring to it. My mom will like it. Can you believe she's sitting with Mr. Suleiman? And look at the way she's glowing. It's extraordinary. She hasn't been on a single date in twenty years as far as I know."

"A Christmas miracle?" Sam smiled. Ronnie's mom looked so happy basking in the radiant adoration of her charming companion.

"I don't know what it is but I'm thanking my lucky stars she's not casting daggers at my dad. It was so wonderful that he could be here to walk me down the aisle. I'll never forget today as long as I live."

Sam kissed her on the cheek, her own hot tears

streaming once again. "Me neither."

"Stop crying!" Ronnie commanded. "You're ruining your makeup." She used a thumb to neaten it. You'd better get up there right now for your own ceremony. Osman looks sensational in a tux."

"Doesn't he?" Osman was talking to friends on the opposite side of the garden, doing his best to stay away from her—at her request—until their ceremony began. He kept glancing up at her, though. He really was the best looking man on the planet. And he was hers!

Emotion welled inside her and threatened to spill over again. Uh-oh, she'd better get up there and get this over with before her dress split open. Her dad was already in position, waiting to lead her up the aisle.

Sam sucked in a deep breath, hoping she could hold it together long enough to get through her vows. Her dad smiled and took her arm.

"Is Mom okay?" Her mom looked fabulous, as usual, in a suit cut to hide her bump, but it was hard to tell with an actress.

"Right as rain." Her dad patted her arm. He probably wouldn't tell her the truth anyway. It hadn't been easy growing up with people who lived in a world of illusion. Maybe that's why she'd started making documentaries—an endless quest for factual evidence in a world where the truth shifted daily. "You look lovely, sweetheart."

"Thanks." She smiled. "Is my mascara all over my face?"

"No. You look perfect. Which doesn't surprise me as you have your mother's beauty."

Sam sighed. Her parents really did seem to love

each other after all these years. Which was surprising since they were at each other's throats more often than not. Maybe that kept things exciting. "How many years have you and Mom been married?"

"Far too many." He winked. "But not nearly enough. You know I can't utter the truth in public as then people will know your mom is older than she claims."

Sam laughed. "Too true!"

The music started, a beautiful nineteenth century wedding march she'd admired for years and always hoped to have at her own ceremony. And here she was! Her true wedding had been an impromptu immersion in Ubarite culture, but this was the one she'd dreamed of since she was a little girl.

She choked back happy tears and took her dad's arm, before walking down the aisle with the hem of her long, poufy dress trailing behind her.

They said the traditional vows they'd written together, Osman so serious and proud, and herself so breathless and emotional that she jumbled her words together. When she finally said, "I do," she wanted to collapse with relief—but she reminded herself that she couldn't even take a deep breath in her beautiful but super-tight dress.

When Osman kissed her, she ached to melt into him, but restrained herself in front of all these people, many of who were seeing her for the first time. It was sometimes hard to remember that she was a queen now, and had to behave with appropriate decorum, so groping the king had to wait for a non-ceremonial occasion.

"What are you laughing at?" Osman saw her funny expression.

"Everything. My whole life. How I'm here right now with you, when a few months ago I could never have imagined anything more outlandish than moving to a faraway country and marrying its king."

"I love you, Samantha Al Kilanjar."

"I love you, too, Osman Al Kilanjar." Emotion swelled her chest until she worried her dress might burst. "And I intend to spend a very long and happy life with you."

The crowd pressed around to offer congratulations, which made tears prick her eyes again, but Sam was relieved when Ronnie suggested that they step away for a few minutes so she could change out of her too-tight dress.

Ronnie insisted on stopping by her own room to pick something up, and when they reached Sam's room and closed the door behind them, she whipped it out from the folds of her dress.

Sam stared at the colorful box. "A pregnancy test?"

"You're very emotional." Ronnie lifted a brow.

"It's my wedding. Of course I'm emotional. Aren't you?" Her voice rose as she spoke. It's not like there was something wrong with having strong feelings at your own wedding, with all your family gathered around you.

"Take it. Prove me wrong." Ronnie thrust it at her.

Sam took it and examined the box. A plus sign for yes, and a minus sign for no.

"But first we'll need to get your dress off, or you'll lose the stick in all the tulle under your skirt."

"It's a miracle the zipper didn't burst. My chest has been heaving with happy tears since I put it on."

Ronnie fiddled with the zipper, easing it down

slowly so it wouldn't break. Sam inhaled and let out a huge sigh of relief. "I don't know how I managed to gain that much weight so quickly."

Ronnie chuckled. "Take the test."

"All right. I'll take it for you. I bet I'm not, though. I'd just *know*. I'm sure of it."

Ronnie cocked her head, and stood there with her arms crossed. Sam hurried into the bathroom in her underwear. She read the teeny print of the directions on the packet. This was silly! Their wedding reception was going on right now. She should be downstairs entertaining her guests.

"Did you do it yet?" called Ronnie through the door.

"You're so impatient. Give me a minute." She managed to fumble the stick out of its wrapping and followed the directions. Of course now she was going to be crushed when it came back negative. She really shouldn't get her hopes up on an important day like today. And what was the rush, anyway? Her biological clock was hardly ready to sound an alarm. She had plenty of time.

"I'm waiting!" Ronnie's singsong voice annoyed her. "Bring it out here. We can watch it together."

"You're nuts." Sam opened the door and walked out. She'd probably done it all wrong. The little circle wasn't changing color at all.

Ronnie peered at the stick. "And you're pregnant."

9

"What?" Sam held it up to her eyes. A tiny pink cross now filled the circle.

"I knew it. It's not like you to sob your mascara off over nothing."

"*Nothing?* Besides, I almost never wear mascara." Sam stared at the plus sign on the stick. "How do we know this is accurate?"

"I have four more of them in my bedroom. Would you like me to get one?"

Sam bit her lip. She didn't need another test. "No." She looked up at Ronnie, whose eyes shone. "You were right. *I'm pregnant.*" The last two words came out in a rasping whisper. Then she grinned. "I can't wait to surprise Osman."

"Are you going to tell him right now?"

"I'll have to wait for a private moment. Maybe tonight."

"Your wedding night." Ronnie winked.

"Yes." She tucked the stick away in her underwear drawer. "So until then we have to act like nothing is different, okay?"

"Okay."

Mackenzie Malone had never experienced anything

like this party. The reception took place in the garden, where guests gathered under the orchard trees. The butterflies were everywhere, perching on people's champagne glasses and fluttering around their heads.

Growing up in small-town Texas, the fanciest affair she ever attended was her cousin Chrissy's wedding where they'd hired the high school band to play for the reception at the local Elks Lodge.

For this double wedding the couples had flown in friends and family from all over the globe—seriously, there were people from India and Africa as well as the U.S.A.—and there must be over a hundred staff waiting on the guests.

She wasn't even supposed to be here. She'd flown into Ubar for a job interview only to be informed on arrival by HR that the whole country had ground to a standstill for the royal weddings, and that she was invited to attend. She didn't mind. She was between jobs right now and they'd paid for her flights and were putting her up in a brand new hotel near the oil facilities. Her parents were taking care of little Madison, who she'd skyped before she came, so she'd lucked into an all-expenses-paid vacation.

Yes, she'd cried at the wedding. Both couples were so obviously in love, and everyone around them seemed so happy for them. She sighed. Once upon a time she'd dreamed of her own wedding. Nothing fancy like this, but it would have been magical all the same. Hadn't happened though, and her little girl was plenty of consolation for her one failed attempt at a Happy Ever After.

And she'd danced with that super hot guy yesterday. He was local and obviously found having her thrust on him rather awkward, but he'd spoken flawless English and was by far the best looking man she'd ever danced with in her life. She felt a smile sneak across her mouth just thinking about him.

Ahmad was his name, if she'd heard it right. And he was right there on the other side of the room. He'd watched the ceremonies with grim concentration and was now tapping furiously into his phone as if he'd rather be anywhere but here. Obviously royal weddings weren't his thing.

They weren't hers either! She wasn't exactly dressed for this affair. In fact this wasn't a dress at all, but a Victoria's Secret nightgown. Luckily for her it was black and plain enough to pass as a dress, so she'd been wearing it almost non-stop since she arrived.

Mackenzie was interviewing to be a mechanic, so she'd intended to wear khakis and a denim shirt for the interview. She wasn't likely to get the job. She wasn't even sure how she felt about moving out here with her daughter, though the money was really, really good. A year or two would give her enough savings to buy a house back in Texas and change their lives.

The person hiring was named Bubba White, which made him sound like the kind of redneck who'd never have glanced at her resumé if she hadn't shortened her name to Mac so he wouldn't know she was a girl. Most likely she'd be rejected and packed off home sometime tomorrow and would never see anything like this again, so she might as well soak it all in.

The brides shared the first dance with their husbands to seventies disco anthem *These Are the Good Times* and soon everyone joined in, swaying and bopping under the date palms. The atmosphere was festive and a little crazy, as the band—a bunch of bearded guys in long robes—kept lurching between rousing pop songs and haunting Christmas carols, as if they were the same sort of music just because they were western.

Once again she was alone, a wallflower. It wasn't all that embarrassing because everyone was too busy to notice, but she was a little sad not to join in the fun. If only she had the nerve to approach Amahd again.

Heck, why not? She'd never see him again, so what did it matter?

What was the worst that could happen? He'd say no. How big of a deal was that?

Screwing up her courage, she peeled herself away from the column she'd been propping up and launched across the floor. Unlike the other women here, she wasn't teetering on heels, because she'd hardly have needed those for an interview as a mechanic. She wore a pair of black roman sandals she'd worn to be comfortable on the plane.

He glanced up suddenly, which made her breath hitch. He must have felt her eyes on him. He stared at her for a moment, as if wondering who she was, then frowned.

Panic flashed through her. Abort mission! Or was he encouraging her? There was something intense in his gaze that told her to keep going. Someone tapped him on the shoulder—a staff member—and he turned to speak with him.

Adrenaline pumping, she marched forward. She was only about twenty feet away, so in less than a minute she'd either be dancing with a handsome man or slinking away with her tail between her legs.

"Hi." He'd gone back to his phone and hadn't

seen her approach.

He looked up, startled. "Hello." His dark eyes were fringed with ridiculously long dark eyelashes but nothing about him looked girly. His jaw was hard as granite and his features bold and commanding. He was obviously friendly with the royals here and possibly pretty important.

Still, she was a free American and could talk to whomever she wanted, right? "I'm Mackenzie, from yesterday. We danced together."

He still hadn't said anything, but at this point she was sure he recognized her. In fact his blistering dark gaze darted to her bust for a split second. Normally that kind of thing would annoy her, but in this instance she took it as strictly encouraging.

"I was wondering," she swallowed. Was she really about to ask a guy to dance? You could probably get thrown out of Texas for something like that.

"Would you do me the honor of dancing with me?" His request pre-empted hers, saving her all kinds of embarrassment and making her want to sing with relief. He was probably just being a gentleman, but that only made her like him more.

"I'd love it." She smiled and took his arm. The band had segued clunkily from "Silent Night" to Michael Jackson's "Thriller", so this time they wouldn't actually have to hold onto each other.

Shame.

Good lord he was handsome. Dressed in a black tuxedo with a bow tie—just like the gorgeous grooms—Amahd was by far the most elegant man she'd ever spoken to. And she wouldn't run into anyone like him back in the Texas oil fields, so she might as well enjoy the view.

They gyrated next to each other, which was kind of funny, since he was obviously rather serious and she was a tomboy rather than a disco diva. He even shot her a sweetly encouraging smile that filled her chest with warmth and made her glad she'd taken a chance and come over.

Now that she wasn't pressed up against him she could appreciate his height—over six foot—and the broad-shouldered, athletic body hidden under all that well-cut cloth. Right now she could soak up enough material to fill her daydreams for five solid years! Which was a good thing as with a demanding job (hopefully soon) and a toddler she didn't have the time or energy to date.

Her heart sank when the song drew to a close. Was he going to rush off again? She wouldn't be mad if he did. It was sweet of him to ask her to dance and she wouldn't act spoiled and hope for more.

Sam, the girl who'd first introduced them, walked out into the middle of the room, clanging a spoon against a champagne glass. She looked resplendent in a long, blue beaded dress—her tan complexion sparkling and her long, dark hair in an elegant updo—every bit the wife of a king. Mac knew she could never look like that in a million years, which was fine, since she had no desire whatsoever to be a king's wife.

Amahd hadn't moved. Which was kind of him, since this would have been the perfect opportunity for him to bow out.

"I want to thank you all for being here to share this special day with us." Sam had a clear, ringing voice as if she addressed large assemblies all the time. "It's the first time Christmas has been celebrated here in the palace, and possibly the first time it's been celebrated anywhere with this many butterflies and goats."

There was a pale yellow goat still running through the crowds. Mac had caught a glimpse of it right in the middle of the second wedding ceremony. That was the kind of thing that would happen at one of her family's weddings, though maybe with pigs or chickens instead. She grinned, feeling strangely at home here.

"I'm sure some of you think it's strange celebrating Christmas in a faraway desert kingdom, but whenever I wonder if I've gone right off the rails—with all my imported mistletoe and forcing the band to learn all the Christmas carols—I remind myself that Christmas started in a desert kingdom and must have once felt rather strange and out of sorts when it first found itself in a Scandinavian log home or a saltbox in colonial Massachusetts."

Sam paused and surveyed the gathered crowd, happiness radiating from her bright smile. "What makes Christmas…well, Christmas, is the people. It's a time when we gather together with family and friends and celebrate hope at the darkest time of the year. We plan to make this an annual tradition, and while I don't imagine you'll all be able to come every year, please know that you are most welcome!"

The crowd clapped and cheered enthusiastically. "I have one more Christmassy request, if you'll all indulge me." Sam looked around. "As you can see, we brought in some mistletoe, and within weeks it's already gotten rather out of hand. You'd be doing us a big favor if you'd reach your hand, pluck a sprig of it—and kiss someone under it."

Whoops of joy exploded from the crowd, and hands reached out to grab at the leafy branches decorating the arches around them, and sneaking up into nearby trees.

Mackenzie hesitated. *Did she dare?*

Amahd was standing there looking rather regal and awkward, as usual. He certainly wasn't going to do anything.

Yes, she dared.

She saw an untouched sprig of the pretty gray-green leaves poking out of a flowerpot nearby. She darted over, snapped off a twig and ran back.

Amahd stared at her as if she'd just lost her mind.

Oh, go on!

She lifted the sprig in the air over his head, which wasn't easy since he was so tall. His gaze jerked to her breasts, which were unfortunately thrust right under his chin, then back up to her face. His eyes dark with mystery and confusion—and possibly desire—he stayed rooted to the spot.

Before he could run away, or she could lose her nerve, she angled her lips up, stood on tiptoes...and realized she couldn't quite reach.

An embarrassed blush was starting to heat her skin when she felt his lips lower over hers.

Shock mingled with relief and she kissed him back. She only wanted a quick peck! She didn't even know the guy.

Holy Toledo. Something was happening. Sensation rushed through her like freshly tapped crude oil.

She could feel his hand on her waist, then sliding lower to cup her backside. Excitement sizzled as she found her own fingers reaching along his hard jaw and up into his thick hair.

Her breasts stirred in her flimsy dress and she pushed herself against his chest, enjoying the hard wall of muscle. Their kiss deepened, tongues finding each other and hot flashes of...something...roaming through her.

She was jerked back to reality when the band launched into a rousing rendition of "Rudolf the Red Nosed Reindeer". Forgotten, the sprig of mistletoe had fallen to the floor and her hands were fisted into his hair. His were on her rear, and the two of them stood pressed against each other—right in the middle of the dance floor.

She wasn't sure who sprang back first. Possibly they did it at the exact same time. Either way, they were both embarrassed! She'd been hoping for a quick dance, then a chaste peck, not a full-on groping session in the middle of a crowded party where she didn't even know anyone!

"You are very beautiful." Amahd bowed his head slightly. His eyes were dark with passion and his lips damp from kissing. "I hope you can excuse my indiscretion."

Very beautiful? No one had ever told her that before. She blinked, still stunned as he turned and vanished into the crowd. From the sound of his apology he blamed himself for the kiss, when of course it was entirely her fault.

Still, it was pretty damn wonderful! This was turning out to be some business trip. She glanced around her and hurried off the dance floor for the safety of a shadowy colonnade. Hopefully no one had noticed their...*indiscretion*.

But all the same, she wasn't likely to forget it as long as she lived.

Sam was beyond thrilled with the progression of the day's events. The mistletoe had proved itself worth the trouble when everyone kissed under it. She could swear she'd even seen Amahd kissing that redhead from yesterday, but maybe her eyes deceived her since there was so much going on. Yes, she'd gone off the deep end a little with both the Christmas festivities and the double wedding, but everyone was having such a great time that all her hard work had already paid off in a lifetime of unforgettable memories.

Dinner was a grand sit-down affair in the largest chamber, with numerous courses of local delicacies served on silver and gold platters. There was some horror and consternation when it was finally discovered that the tender delicacy the chef had used to replace the rescued goats was actually bulls' testicles, but everyone recovered enough to enjoy the dessert made of spun honey and rose wine.

By the end of the long and emotional day, Sam was bursting to tell Osman her news, and it was well after midnight when they finally found themselves alone in their bedroom.

Osman untied the sash around his waist. "Are you tired my love?"

"A little." How much could she tease him?

He unbuttoned his shirt and shucked off his pants, revealing his strong, tan body. "It's been a long day." Mischief and desire gleamed in his eyes as he strode toward her. "But I still have plenty of energy left."

"Oh, do you?" She lifted a brow as a smile crept across her mouth. "What a surprise."

Osman took the hem of her dress between his

thumb and forefinger and lifted it over her head in one swift movement that left her dressed in her blue bra and panties.

"What a sight for sore eyes," he murmured. "I've been dreaming of this moment all day. It was a challenge having to share you with so many people."

Sam hesitated. "You're going to have to share me with one more person." It was hard keeping a straight face.

He frowned. "Who?"

"Take a guess."

"Your parents are moving here? I'm so glad. I'd love to have more family around us."

"No! On both counts. I love my parents but I love them best when they're thousands of miles away from me. Someone…younger than me. But still a relative."

"You have a sibling? A brother or sister you never told me about?" Confusion furrowed his royal brow.

She shook her head mysteriously. "Keep guessing."

He glanced at her belly, and she realized with a jolt that her hand had unconsciously wandered there.

"A baby," he breathed.

She smiled. "Yes. Ronnie made me take a test this afternoon. And she was right, all my tears and hysteria and manic organizing of festivities can now be blamed on hormonal upheaval."

Osman stared at her, first her face, then her belly, then her face again. "A baby. Our child."

He took her in his arms and she could feel his chest heaving with emotion. "I love you so much, Sam. And I look forward to sharing you with our son or daughter. I promise you I'll be the best father I can be." Emotion cracked his voice.

Osman's own father had been a tyrant who thought of nothing but his own pleasure, quietly killing his wives when he was done with them and packing his lonely sons off to distant boarding schools. She knew Osman was determined to be a real father, who shared his life with his children and loved and enjoyed them.

"I know you will." She kissed him, soft and gentle at first, then more passionately, as she let the emotion and excitement of the day flow between them like electric current.

"This is the best Christmas present ever," he whispered, when their lips finally parted.

"Can you see why I wanted to bring Christmas to a country where it's never really existed?"

"I can. Everyone is enjoying it so much."

"And Christmas did start in the desert, after all. When a baby was born in a manger and three wise men set out on camels to follow a star."

"I still don't understand what that has to do with fir trees with glass balls on them."

"Or mistletoe. Or a bearded man with a sack of gifts for that matter." She smiled. "Christmas is rather like a snowball rolling down a hill, gathering up all the traditions that came before it and incorporating them so that it feels welcoming to everyone."

"Or like these butterflies." Osman looked at a pretty one fluttering near their bedside lamp. "That adapt to a new environment and make themselves at home."

He kissed her again, long and soft and slow. "Merry Christmas, my queen. I look forward to celebrating many of them with you…" He glanced at her belly, and she could see the emotion in his face.

"And our family."

Her heart was so full she could hardly bear it. "Merry Christmas to you, too, my love." She smiled and stroked his rough cheek. "But now we'd better get some sleep because the guys I hired to play the wise men on camels are arriving before dawn and I need to figure out which of those smelly boxes is frankincense and which is myrrh. Oh, and I'd better coach Rifal on how to play Santa for all the little kids, and I have to make sure they use a quiet donkey for the manger scene, not one that will kick, and—"

"Don't worry, Sam. I have a feeling it will be the merriest Christmas in the history of the world."

She could see his chest shaking with laughter. "I know you think I'm crazy."

"You are crazy." He gazed at her, eyes shining. "And I'm crazy in love with you."

THE END

Explore all of the *Desert Kings* stories:

Novella: Veronica–Stranded with the Sheikh

Book 1: Osman–Rescued by the Sheikh

Book 2: Zadir–Bought for the Sheikh

Novella: A Christmas wedding

Book 3: Gibran–Return of the Rebel Sheikh

Book 4: Amahd–Captivated by the Sheikh

ABOUT THE AUTHOR

Jennifer Lewis loves heat in all its forms including spicy food, steamy temperatures and smoking hot heroes. She is a USA TODAY bestselling author and her books have been translated into more than twenty languages. She lives in sunny South Florida and when she's not sitting at her laptop she can often be found at the beach. Read more about her books and join her new release mailing list at www.jenlewis.com.